CHILDREN OF ST. MARTHA
Y

973 But
Butler, Daphne
   U.S.A

ON THE MAP

U.S.A.

Titles in This Series:

France

Italy

Spain

U.S.A.

Series editor: Daphne Butler
American editor: Marian L. Edwards
Design: M&M Partnership
Photographs: ZEFA except 15 (bottom) Isaac Geib/Grant Heilman Photography
Map artwork: Raymond Turvey
Cover photo: *Downtown Dallas, Texas*

Copyright © text 1993 Steck-Vaughn Company

All rights reserved. No part of the material protected by this copyright may be reproduced or utilized in any form or by any means, electronic or mechanical, including photocopying, recording, or by any information storage and retrieval system, without permission in writing from the copyright owner. Requests for permission to make copies of any part of the work should be mailed to: Copyright Permissions, Steck-Vaughn Company, P.O. Box 26015, Austin, TX 78755

Library of Congress Cataloging-in-Publication Data

Butler, Daphne, 1945–
   USA / Daphne Butler.
     p.   cm. — (On the map)
   Includes index.
   Summary: Provides an overview of life in the United States, covering the country's physical features, natural resources, city life, education, famous landmarks, and more.
   ISBN 0-8114-3676-4
   1. United States — Juvenile literature. [1. United States.]
I. Title. II. Series.
E156.B88 1992   92–13647
973—dc20   CIP
                                             AC

Typeset by Multifacit Graphics, Keyport, NJ
Printed and bound in the United States.

1 2 3 4 5 6 7 8 9 0 VH 98 97 96 95 94 93

U.S.A.

Daphne Butler

RAINTREE
STECK-VAUGHN
PUBLISHERS
The Steck-Vaughn Company

Austin, Texas

Contents

A Big Country	6–7
Mountains and Deserts	8–9
Rivers, Lakes, and Swamps	10–11
The Fifty States	12–13
Natural Resources	14–15
Life in the United States	16–17
Going to School	18–19
Getting Around	20–21
Using the Land	22–23
Living in the City	24–25
Playing Hard	26–27
Famous Landmarks	28–29
Facts and Figures	30
Further Reading	31
Index	32

Snowplow clearing snow from a highway in Alaska.

Rice growing in California. Some of the world's best farmland is in California.

Beaver pond in the Glacier National Park, Montana.

A mat and hat maker at work near the shore in sunny Florida.

A Big Country

The United States of America, also called the U.S.A. or United States, is a very large country. It is one of the largest countries in the world. The United States is on the continent of North America. It shares the continent with two other countries.

This huge country lies between two oceans. In the west the United States borders the Pacific Ocean. In the east, it borders the Atlantic. The distance between east and west is so great that the sun rises about three hours later on the West Coast than on the East Coast.

In the north, the United States shares a border with Canada, and in the south with Mexico. But there is much more to the United States. Alaska is in the upper Northwest, and Hawaii is in the Pacific. In addition, the United States has possession of islands in the Caribbean Sea and the Pacific Ocean.

A variety of climates and weather can be found throughout the country. Alaska, in the north, is bitterly cold in winter. Florida, in the south, is warm year-round. The southwest is hot and dry, while the middle of the country gets plenty of rainfall in summer and snow in winter.

Mountains and Deserts

The United States is a beautiful country. Part of the beauty is the land. From coast to coast, there are many different land areas. Ranges of high mountains run down the west side of the United States. A much smaller range runs down the east side. In between, flat prairies and treeless plains stretch for hundreds of miles.

Mountains are the highest places on the earth. Some mountains are bare and rocky near the top. Some are covered by thick forests. Still others level off into plateaus of high hills and deep valleys. In some places the land levels off and is barren for miles around. Odd-shaped rock formations, caused by the wind and sand, stand out from the rest.

A few areas of the United States get very little rain or snow during the year. The weather is hot and dry. These places are called deserts. They are mostly found in the West and the Southwest. Since it is so dry in the desert, many plants cannot live. But some plants can grow. They have a special way to store water.

Today people have found ways to bring water to some desert areas. They irrigate the soil and make it good for growing crops.

The Guadalupe Mountains, New Mexico.

Rivers, Lakes, and Swamps

Many rivers began as tiny mountain streams. These streams are fed by snow and ice. They flow off the mountains, join together, and run down to the sea.

The United States has many rivers. The Mississippi River is the largest. In places the Mississippi is over three and one-half miles wide. The Missouri River is the second largest river in the United States. The two rivers meet and form the massive Mississippi-Missouri River system. It drains water from the prairies into the Gulf of Mexico.

In the north, a chain of five huge lakes form part of the border between the United States and Canada. These are known as the Great Lakes. They are the most important lakes in the country.

The Great Lakes are connected to one another. Lake Ontario, the smallest of the Great Lakes, is almost the size of New Jersey. Lake Superior is the largest. It is a little larger than South Carolina.

Swamplands are found mostly in the South. The most famous swamp is the Everglades in Florida. It is an area rich with plants and animals.

The Mississippi River at New Orleans, Louisiana.

An airboat trip in Everglades National Park, Florida.

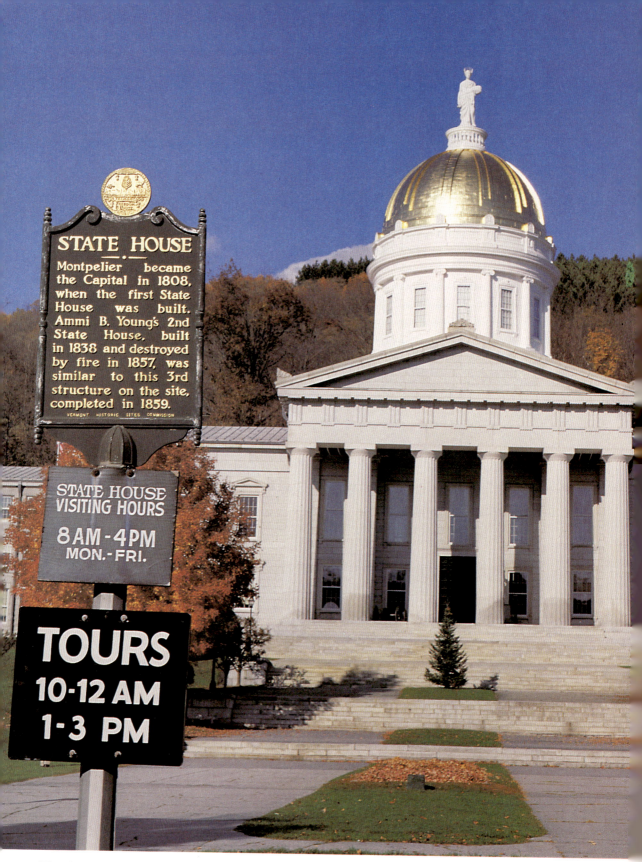

The State House in Montpelier, Vermont.

The Fifty States

The United States is made up of 50 separate states. Each state can govern itself in some ways. In other ways it is managed by the federal government in Washington, D.C.

Washington is the capital of the United States. It is located in the District of Columbia, a small area of land set aside by the government. The government in Washington manages the whole country.

Each state in the United States has its own government and capital city. States make laws and have control over their own schools, colleges, and police forces. The governor is the leader of a state. The governor's job is to manage the state and make sure that all the state's laws are followed.

Delaware, Hawaii, and Rhode Island are small states. Texas, California, and Alaska are very large. In fact, they are larger than some countries in other parts of the world.

In what state do you live? What is the name of the capital city of your state? Look at the map. Is your state large, small, or in-between?

Natural Resources

The United States is rich in natural resources. It has good farmland, thick forests, and plenty of fresh water. Large deposits of minerals, including coal, oil, and natural gas, lie under the ground. These resources have helped to make the United States the wealthiest country in the world.

The American people are creative and hardworking. The United States has been a world leader in the production of goods and services. The big industrial cities in the North and East produce a wide range of products. These products are shipped to all parts of the world.

While rich farmland is found in almost every state, the largest farms are in the South, Midwest, and West. Here enough food is grown to feed all Americans, with plenty left over to trade with other countries. In addition, the United States sends food to many poor countries that cannot feed themselves.

Along the northern Pacific Coast and in the Southeast, thick forests have helped make wood an important product. There are many companies that make things from wood such as furniture and paper.

Pumping oil in California. Oil is an important part of the economy.

Chicago, Illinois at night. Chicago plays an important part in trade across the U.S.

A corn harvest in the Midwest.

Disney World in Florida—a fantasy theme park known throughout the world.

Life in the United States

Americans enjoy one of the world's highest standards of living. They have the freedom to choose their own way of life. Living in America, people have the right to pick the places they want to live and the kinds of work they want to do.

Americans are hard workers who take pride in their jobs and their homes. The money they earn is used to buy the things they want and need. But Americans save some of their money, too. They save for their children's education. Americans want their children to have even better lives than they do.

People in America like to have a good time. They enjoy time away from school and jobs. Many take a vacation each year. Some people like to visit other places. Others stay at home and enjoy the time with their family and friends.

In the United States, schools and offices open early in the day and close in late afternoon. Shops, stores, and restaurants are open until late in the evening. Some never close. A wide variety of foods and other goods can be found in many stores and shops. It is the wonderful variety—from tacos and burritos to lasagna and pizza—that makes it interesting.

American parents like their children to have a practical education. They see it as the first step towards a good job.

Going to School

Every state has a public school system. Public schools offer a free education to all children. Most public school systems have facilities for all levels of schooling from preschool through high school education.

American children are required to attend school. It is an important part of their lives. They must go to school until they reach a certain age or grade.

Children first start in preschool or nursery school before going to kindergarten. Usually by age six, children attend first grade. After completing elementary school, they go to junior high and high school. Besides getting a practical education, today's schools also offer classes in physical education, music, and computers.

Once out of high school, students can continue their education. Some may go to a college or university. Others choose a vocational school. There they learn a special trade or job, such as electrician, chef, mechanic, or hairdresser. Whatever the choice, Americans encourage their children to continue their education after high school.

Getting Around

People in the United States are always on the move. They like to travel from place to place. The most popular way of getting around is by car. Americans use their cars for driving to work, shopping, and to visit other places. Comfortable cars, safe highways, and bridges make driving enjoyable to many.

Some people like to use public transportation to get around a town or city. Buses and subways are examples of public transportation. Buses are the leading mass transit vehicle. They are the favorite way of getting around in a city.

Buses also travel over long distances. They carry people from city to city or from state to state. Many people like to take bus trips across the entire country. A bus trip is a good way to relax and see the country.

People who need to get from one place to another fast, can take a train or an airplane. These are fast and provide good service to passengers.

What kind of trips do you take? What is your favorite way to travel? What are some other ways people travel from one place to another?

The freeway outside of San Francisco, California.
The U.S. has many thousands of miles of highways and roads.

Buses are a comfortable and relaxing way to travel from place to place.

Highways cross vast unpopulated areas.
Oak Creek Canyon, Arizona.

Using the Land

About half of the land in the United States is good farmland. All kinds of crops are grown. Some farms specialize or grow only one kind of crop. Often fields of the same crop stretch for many miles.

Many farms grow mixed crops. That is, they grow several kinds of fruits or vegetables. The kind of crops grown depends on the climate. Crops like wheat, corn, and soybean are important for world trade.

Most of the oranges and grapefruits in the United States are grown in California and Florida. These states also grow green vegetables. In the middle of the country grains such as wheat, barley, and corn are common sights. Cotton and rice are just a few of the crops that grow well in the South and Southwest.

Some of the land in the United States is used for raising chickens and cattle. Chicken farms can be seen all along the East Coast from Maryland to South Carolina. The cattle industry is big in the Midwest and Southwest.

Whether growing crops or raising chickens or cattle, the land in the United States is one of the most productive in the world.

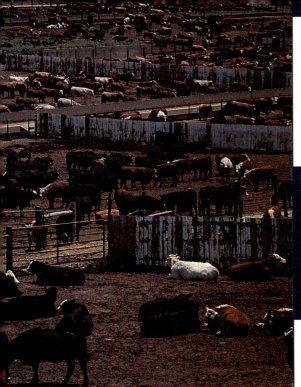

Cattle ready for market in Dodge City, Kansas.

Cotton picking in Arizona.

Wheat grows in the Midwest.

San Francisco, California—a pleasing mix of old and new buildings.

New York City is the largest city in the United States.

An elegant shopping mall in Baltimore, Maryland.

New Orleans, Louisiana—the birthplace of jazz.

Living in the City

Large cities, also known as urban areas, are surrounded by small towns and suburbs. Cities are often built on a grid pattern. That is, the streets cross at right angles that form blocks. A block may have different kinds of buildings. There are apartment buildings, office buildings, stores, and shops.

Skyscrapers are very tall buildings. They tower over the buildings around them. Some skyscrapers are apartment buildings where people live. Some are headquarters of large companies.

Cities are exciting places to live. There are so many things to do. People have a variety of stores, restaurants, museums, and theaters to choose from. There are huge open fruit markets and luxury department stores. Cities also offer a wide selection of goods and services.

Many different kinds of things are made in cities. These include food products, clothing, toys, and jewelry. Also books, newspapers, and magazines are often made in the city. These goods are not only used by Americans, they are also shipped to distant parts of the world.

Playing Hard

Americans enjoy all kinds of sports. All across the country people are active in sports. These may range from boating to bowling and from skiing to surfing. People work hard at sports because they are fun and good for their health.

Sports also provide entertainment. Americans enjoy watching college and professional team sports. Baseball, basketball, football, and hockey are national games. Many people go to games to see their favorite teams play. Fans follow their favorite teams on radio or watch them on television.

Special places such as arenas, stadiums, and clubs are found throughout the United States. Large crowds will brave all kinds of weather to attend some sports events. They will sit in drenching rain or freezing snow to watch their favorite team play.

Most Americans love the people who play sports. They become fans of the athletes. Many athletes have become rich and famous. They are national celebrities. Young people often look up to a successful athlete.

What kind of sports do you like to play? What are your favorite team sports? Name your favorite athletes.

Off the Wall Skatepark, Point Pleasant Beach, New Jersey.

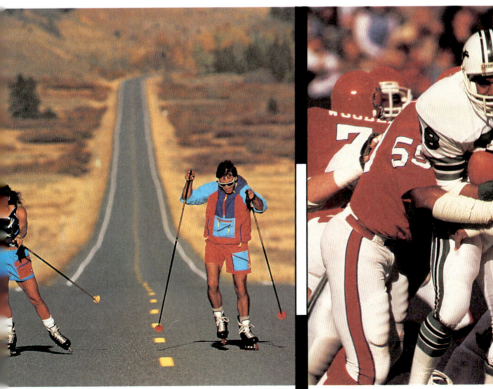

Roller skaters on a backcountry road in Idaho.

Football is a rough sport. Players need protective equipment.

Famous Landmarks

The Statue of Liberty, in New York, was a gift from France to the U.S. It is a symbol of friendship and liberty.

The Grand Canyon, Arizona. This vast canyon is 217 miles long, 18 miles wide, and up to 1 mile deep.

Death Valley, California. Temperatures in summer reach 134°F, making it the hottes place in the United States.

The heads of Presidents Washington, Jefferson, Theodore Roosevelt, and Lincoln. Mt. Rushmore, South Dakota.

Sears Tower in Chicago, Illinois is the tallest building in the world. It is 110 stories (1,454 feet) tall.

The Capitol building in Washington, D.C. This is the home of the U.S. government.

The Cliff Palace in the Mesa Verde National Park, Colorado—buildings from an ancient Native American culture.

Facts and Figures

U.S.A.-The Land and People

Population	248,710,000
Area	3,615,191 square miles
Capital city	Washington, D.C.
Largest city Population	New York 7,322,564
Language	English
Religion	Christian—but all religions practiced
Money	Dollars $1 = 100 cents
Highest mountain	Mt. McKinley 20,320 feet
Longest river	Mississippi-Missouri 3,740 miles

Main Public Holidays

New Year's Day	January 1
Martin L. King Day	3rd Monday in January
Lincoln's birthday	February 12
Washington's birthday or Presidents' Day	3rd Monday in February
Memorial Day	last Monday in May
Independence Day	July 4
Labor Day	1st Monday in September
Columbus Day	2nd Monday in October
Veterans' Day	November 11
Thanksgiving Day	4th Thursday in November
Christmas Day	December 25

The States

Alabama	Montana
Alaska	Nebraska
Arizona	Nevada
Arkansas	New Hampshire*
California	New Jersey*
Colorado	New Mexico
Connecticut*	New York*
Delaware*	North Carolina*
Florida	North Dakota
Georgia*	Ohio
Hawaii	Oklahoma
Idaho	Oregon
Illinois	Pennsylvania*
Indiana	Rhode Island*
Iowa	South Carolina*
Kansas	South Dakota
Kentucky	Tennessee
Louisiana	Texas
Maine	Utah
Maryland*	Vermont
	Virginia*
Massachusetts*	Washington
Michigan	West Virginia
Minnesota	Wisconsin
Mississippi	Wyoming
Missouri	

*original 13 States

Average Temperatures in Fahrenh[eit]

City and State	January	Ju[ly]
Barrow, Alaska (north)	-18°F	39°
New York, New York (east)	32°F	73°
Miami, Florida (south)	67°F	82°
San Francisco, California (west)	49°F	58°

Further Reading

Aten, Jerry. *America: From Sea to Shining Sea.* Good Apple, 1988.

———. *Fifty Nifty States.* Good Apple, 1990.

Aylesworth, Thomas G. *Kids' World Almanac of the United States,* Pharos Books, NY, 1990.

Beck, Michael and Scott, Judy. *Getting into Geography: The States and Flags Through Research and Activities.* Skippingstone Press, 1990.

Brandt, Sue R. *Facts about the Fifty States,* second rev. edition, Watts, 1988.

Caney, Steven. *Steven Caney's Kids' America.* Workman Publishing Co., 1978.

Cobblestone Publishing, Inc. Staff. *U.S. History Cartoons: For Young People.* Cobblestone Publishing, 1987.

James, Ian. *United States.* Watts, 1990.

Somerville, L. *First Book of America.* Educational Development Corp., 1990.

Index

buildings 25
  Capitol 29
  Cliff Castle 29
  restaurants 17
  Sears Tower 29
  skyscrapers 25
  shopping mall 24
  shops 17

Canada 7, 10
canyons 8
  Grand Canyon 28
  Oak Creek Canyon 21
cattle 22, 23
cities 14, 25
  Baltimore 24
  Chicago 15, 29
  Dodge City 23
  Montpelier 12
  New Orleans 11, 24
  New York 24, 28
  San Francisco 21, 24
  Washington 13, 29
crops 22
  barley 22
  corn 22
  cotton 22, 23
  grains 22
  oranges 22
  rice 6, 22
  vegetables 22
  wheat 22, 23

deserts 8
  Death Valley 28
Disney World 16
District of Columbia 13, 29

farmland 6, 14, 22
food 14, 17
forest 8

geysers 8
government 13
grassland 8
Gulf of Mexico 10

lakes 10
  Great Lakes 10
  Lake Superior 10
  salt lakes 8

Mexico 7
mountains 8, 10
  Guadalupe Mountains 9
  Mount Rushmore 29
  Mount McKinley 30

National Parks
  Everglades 11
  Glacier 6
  Mesa Verde 29

oceans 7
  Atlantic 7
  Pacific 7

prairies 8, 10

rivers 10
  Mississippi 11
  Mississippi-Missouri 10

school 13, 17, 19
sports 26
  baseball 26
  clubs 26
  football 26, 27
  roller skaters 27
  skate-boarding 27
  sports centers 26
  stadiums 26
States 13, 30
  Alaska 6, 7, 13
  Arizona 21, 28
  California 6, 13, 21, 22, 24, 28
  Colorado 29
  Delaware 13
  Florida 6, 7, 10, 11, 16, 22
  Hawaii 7, 13
  Idaho 27
  Illinois 15, 29
  Kansas 23
  Louisiana 11, 24
  Maryland 13, 24
  Montana 6
  Nebraska 23
  New Jersey 10, 27
  New Mexico 9
  South Carolina 10
  South Dakota 29
  Vermont 12
Statue of Liberty 28
swamp 10
  Everglades 10

trade 14, 15, 22
  goods 14
travel
  bus 20, 21
  cars 20
  freeway 20, 21
  highway 6, 21
  plane 20
  snowplow 6
  train 20

wealth 25, 26
  goods 14
  job 18
  minerals 14
  oil 15
  trade 14, 15, 22
  work 17
weather 7
  ice 8
  snow 8

©1991 Simon & Schuster Young Books

Date Due

JAN 7 '93			
FEB 3 '94			
FEB 24 '94			
MAR 10 '94			
SEP 20 '94			

```
917.3     Butler, Daphne
But       U.S.A.
```

15.75

**CHILDREN OF ST. MARTHA
SCHOOL LIBRARY**